GIRLS F.C.

1 4 [...] **Pielichaty** (pronounced Pierre-li-hatty)
[wri]tten numerous books for children, including
[...]e's *Letters*, which was nominated for the
[Carn]egie Medal. Football has often been a theme
[in H]elena's writing, beginning with *There's Only*
[On]e Danny Ogle (OUP 2000) about a boy who
[hap]pens to support Helena's favourite club,
[Hud]dersfield Town. Helena is a fan of the women's
[ga]me, too, influenced no doubt by her Auntie Pat
[pla]ying for Yorkshire Copperworks in the 1950s.
[Her] daughter also played for various teams from
[the] age of 10 onwards. The Griffins U11s, a local
girls' team, ins[pired] many of the stories in Girls FC.

Do Goalkeepers Wear Tiaras?

Helena Pielichaty

WALKER
BOOKS

**For Robert Tingle and St Oswald's Primary School,
New Longton – a promise kept**

First published 2009 by Walker Books Ltd
This edition published 2018
87 Vauxhall Walk, London SE11 5HJ

10 9 8 7 6 5 4 3 2 1

Text © 2009 Helena Pielichaty
Cover illustration © 2018 Eglantine Ceulemans

The right of Helena Pielichaty to be identified as author
of this work has been asserted by her in accordance with
the Copyright, Designs and Patents Act 1988

This book has been typeset in Helvetica and Handwriter

Printed and bound in Great Britain by CPI Group (UK) Ltd

British Library Cataloguing in Publication Data:
a catalogue record for this book is available from the British Library

ISBN 978-1-4063-8332-4

www.walker.co.uk

MIX
Paper from
responsible sources
FSC
www.fsc.org   FSC® C020471

The Team

⚽ **Megan "Meggo" Fawcett** GOAL

⚽ **Petra "Wardy" Ward** DEFENCE

⚽ **Lucy "Goose" Skidmore** DEFENCE

⚽ **Dylan "Dyl" or "Psycho 1" McNeil** LEFT WING

⚽ **Holly "Hols" or "Wonder" Woolcock** DEFENCE

⚽ **Veronika "Nika" Kozak** MIDFIELD

⚽ **Jenny-Jane "JJ" or "Hoggy" Bayliss** MIDFIELD

⚽ **Gemma "Hursty" or "Mod" Hurst** MIDFIELD

⚽ **Eve "Akka" Akboh** STRIKER

⚽ **Tabinda "Tabby" or "Tabs" Shah** STRIKER/MIDFIELD

⚽ **Daisy "Dayz" or "Psycho 2" McNeil** RIGHT WING

⚽ **Amy "Minto" or "Lil Posh" Minter** VARIOUS

Official name: Parrs Under 11s, also known as the Parsnips

Ground: Lornton FC, Low Road, Lornton

Capacity: 500

Affiliated to: the Nettie Honeyball Women's League junior division

Sponsors: Sweet Peas Garden Centre, Mowborough

Club colours: red and white; red shirts with white sleeves, white shorts, red socks with white trim

Coach: Hannah Preston

Assistant coach: Katie Regan

Pre-match Interview

Hello. My name is Megan Fawcett and I'm the goalie for the Parrs Under 11s, the best football team in the world. Don't worry if you have never heard of us; I won't be offended. Perhaps you've never heard of Donny Belles or Dick, Kerr's Ladies either? Nothing would surprise me.

Anyway, I am going to kick off the series by explaining how the team got together in the first place. I hope you'll enjoy the story, even if you're a bit weird and don't like football.

Love and penalty saves,
Megan F xxx

It was a Wednesday afternoon and I was sitting in the bottom cloakroom with Tabinda, getting ready for football practice.

I was feeling nervous. I always feel nervous before football practice but today I was more nervous than usual; my hands were trembling.

I don't think Tabinda had noticed. She was busy stuffing her shin pads down her socks, her long dark plaits almost touching the floor as she concentrated. I had already shoved my shin pads down my socks. Now all I had to do was make sure my tiara didn't fall off. "Is this on straight?" I asked.

She nodded, then did a double take and scowled. "What are you doing?" she asked.

"Getting ready for football practice. What are you doing?" I replied.

She frowned at me and didn't say anything for about ten seconds. "OK, Megan, I give in. Why are you wearing fairy wings and a tiara?"

I tugged at the elastic holding my wings together and shrugged. "To see if Mr Glasshouse even notices."

Tabinda understood immediately. "Nice one."

"I thought so."

"Ready, then?"

"Ready."

Together we left the cloakroom and trudged out onto the school field to join the others in the squad, our boots making a click-clicking sound on the floor.

An hour later we left the school field and trudged back into the cloakroom, our boots making a click-clicking sound on the floor. I pulled off the wings and threw the tiara into the bottom of my kit bag and looked at Tabinda.

Tabinda looked at me. "Well, you tried," she said.

"I did," I agreed.

2

The next day I returned the wings and tiara to my best friend, Petra. "Sorry, one of the wings got a bit bent. Reece Gilbert cropped me and I went flying."

Petra laughed and hung the wings off the back of her chair. "Went flying! Good one."

"Oh yeah," I said. I hadn't even realized I'd made a joke. That shows how fed up I was.

"Did it work? Did Mr Glasshouse notice you?" Petra asked.

I shook my head.

She looked at me, her head crooked to one side, the way she does when she's being sympathetic. "Don't give up, Megan. I bet he did notice but just didn't say anything so the others wouldn't get jealous. Bet you anything you'll be on the team this time. Or on the bench at least."

"I won't be," I said. "It's a cup match. He won't risk it."

"Wait until you've seen the noticeboard at break. You never know."

So I went to the noticeboard at break. The team list was up. Mr Glasshouse had even used clip-art of a couple of trophies to decorate it.

The list went like this:

CUP MATCH

ROUND 1:

Mowborough Primary v. St Martin's Primary
Wednesday 7 February, 4.15 p.m.

TEAM:

Boy in Y6	Girl in Y6	Girl in Y6
Boy in Y6	Boy in Y6	Boy in Y6
Boy in Y5		

SUBS:

Boy in Y5	Girl in Y6

Just so you know, I'm in Year Three. So's Tabinda. 'Nuff said.

Petra linked her arm through mine and steered me away from the noticeboard. "My dad's got a sumo outfit from this party he went to at Christmas if you want to try that next time."

"I'll pass," I said, "but thanks."

3

Mum was not that sympathetic when I told her I hadn't made the team. "Well, just keep trying," she said, spooning our cat Whiskas his Whiskas into the cat bowl.

"But I'd just like to know what it feels like to run out onto the pitch against another team. Even for, like, ten minutes or something."

"Yes, well, at least you can run..." Mum began.

Here we go, I thought. My mum's a nurse. Having a mum as a nurse is good for things like if you cut yourself or break something or you wake up covered in yellow crusty blobs. It's not good if you feel sorry for yourself because you haven't made the footy team. "There was a little girl in a wheelchair in A and E this morning," Mum said. "She couldn't have been older than five. Sweet

little thing, but she'll never be able to walk…
She was born with …" Mum came out with this
complicated word ending in "itis".

"You can still play football if you're in a
wheelchair!" I pointed out. "In a gym, not on grass,
obviously, but you can still play. I've seen it on telly."

Mum gave me a bit of a look.

"I'll go and do my homework," I said.

Dad was more understanding. He played football
for his school, right up to Year Eleven, and he still
has a kick-about with the lads down at the station
where he's a fire officer. "That's a shame," he said
when I told him.

"I know."

"Chin up, petal, eh? He's bound to notice the
Fawcett flair at some stage."

So I kept my chin up. I attended football practice
every Wednesday. I wore sensible clothing. I tried as
hard as I could during the drills. I dribbled. I volleyed.

I controlled the ball (most times). I went anywhere I was told during the short matches at the end. I ran and fetched the ball if it went miles out of play – unlike some Year Sixes I could mention. I kept my chin up and my head down.

I might have continued like that right through Year Four, Year Five and into Year Six if it hadn't been for Faye Pratt dropping a brick on her foot.

4

It was half-six in the morning when Dad woke me that fateful Sunday. "Now then, Fishface," he said, "rise and shine."

I squinted at him with one eye. "What? How come?"

"Mum's just phoned; Faye Pratt can't come in to do her shift." Faye Pratt is one of the nurses on Mum's ward.

"Why?"

"She dropped a brick on her foot making a rabbit hutch. Apparently, it looks like a watermelon with a sock on – the foot, not the rabbit hutch. Anyway, Mum's having to stay on until they find a relief nurse, and I'm due down at the station for half-seven, so I've got to take you to Auntie Mandy's."

Auntie Mandy is my emergency babysitter.

She is the manager of the clubhouse at Lornton
FC, a football club about five miles away. I love
going to Auntie Mandy's! There's always so much
happening. I sprang out from under my duvet, took
a quick shower, put on my jeans and England shirt
and dashed downstairs. "Ready when you are,
sonny boy," I said to my dad five minutes later.

He glanced at his watch. "Mm. That might just
be a record."

Like Batman and Robin we leapt into our Volvo
and set off. I'd hardly settled into my seat when
my mobile vibrated. "That'll be your mum," Dad
predicted – but it wasn't Mum's, it was Petra's
picture flashing on the screen. Petra is an early
riser, but before eight o'clock on a Sunday is going
some, even for her. "Are you OK?" I asked.

"Yes," she said. "I didn't think you'd answer.
I was going to leave a message."

"I'm on my way to my auntie Mandy's."

"Oh."

Now when you've known someone since

nursery, you can tell a lot from a simple "oh".
Petra's "oh" was not a happy "oh". "Spill," I said.

She sighed. "Oh, nothing."

"Spill."

She sighed again. "It's just I've got to go with
Mum and Charlotte to some stupid horse thing
miles away. I've been waiting in the back of the car
for about four years for them to load Betty Boo
into the horsebox and sort out the tack. I'm well
fed up. I wish I could hang out with you instead."

Now this was just plain spooky. We'd be going
by the top of Petra's lane in less than half a mile.
"So you fancy spending the day with me instead?"
I asked.

"Well, dur!"

"Can you be standing outside your gate in one
second?"

"Seriously?"

"So seriously."

My phone line went dead.

We picked Petra up, waved to her mum and Charlotte, then set off again. I sent Auntie Mandy a text to tell her about Petra coming and by the time she'd replied saying "No probs" we were already outside the clubhouse waiting for her to open the door.

She answered almost at once, still in her dressing gown, her brown curly hair all over the place. Curly hair runs on that side of the family, only mine and Mum's curls are red. I think Auntie Mandy's should be red, too, but she cheats. "Good morning, Trouble," she said to me and gave me a hug. "And hello to Petra," she said – and gave her a hug too!

I kissed Dad goodbye, then followed Auntie Mandy upstairs, carefully avoiding the empty bottle crates stacked in the entrance-cum-cloakroom and trying not to breathe in the smell of stale beer from the bar. The clubhouse isn't exactly posh. Outside it's a plain brick building, with ball-bashed wire meshing over the downstairs windows and two entrances, one at either end – one for the club and one for the changing rooms.

Inside is better, though, and Auntie Mandy's upstairs flat is small but cosy. We sat for a while in the sunny kitchen eating bacon butties and drinking tea.

"How's school?" Auntie Mandy asked. "Any joy with the football team?"

"Please don't set her off," Petra begged. "She'll moan for hours."

"I will not!" I protested, then began moaning.

"Told you!" Petra grinned, licking tomato ketchup from her fingers.

"Poor Megan! Why don't you go and get a ball from the storeroom and have a kick-around while the place is deserted," Auntie Mandy said.

I didn't need telling twice. I was downstairs and in that storeroom faster than you can say Wayne Rooney rocks.

5

"That's a lot of space," Petra commented as we approached the pitch.

I knew what she meant. A proper football pitch does feel massive when there're only two of you. We stayed by the goalmouth nearest the main path, passing the ball backwards and forwards between us along the white line marking out the six-yard box. Despite the sunshine, the day hadn't warmed up yet and there was a cool breeze ruffling our shirts. "Lordy Wardy! Put some effort in; I'm freezing!"

"Hold your corset, Fawcett!" Petra replied, taking a swipe at the ball, which she totally mis-kicked and sent flying miles behind me.

"Who was that to? A Martian?"

"You wanted to get moving!" she called as

I chased after the ball bobbling towards the dead-ball line. I trapped it with my foot, then dribbled back.

"You're so good!" Petra sighed.

I shrugged. "Yeah, well, so would you be if you joined in at lunchtimes."

"Huh! Tell that to my mum."

Poor Petra. Mrs Ward does like to keep her busy, what with clarinet lessons and choir and maths club and other complete wastes of time. "Come on, let's do something else. Shall we go in goal? You shoot and I save, then swap round?"

Petra glanced towards the goalmouth. "I can't dive or anything; I've got my new jeans on – Mum'll kill me if I tear them."

"I don't mind going in goal all the time."

"Are you sure?"

"Sure I'm sure."

I'd never had a go in goal before – it was the one position that never seemed to fall my way during practices. As I walked towards the goal line,

I realized for the first time how high and wide apart the posts were; I didn't even come halfway up, and the distance from one end to the other was about the same size as my bedroom! I patted the cold white wood. "Kind little post," I told it, "help Megan keep a clean sheet!"

I strode over to the middle of the goal and stood where the goal line should be, but because it was nearing the end of the season, it was just a bare patch of hard, dry mud. Planting my legs firmly where I guessed the line ought to run, I crouched forward, my arms outstretched like I'd seen our school goalie do. "Bring it on!" I called out to Petra, who was placing the ball on the penalty spot.

"Goal number one coming up!" she said, and charged.

I felt a tingle dart through me. My eyes never left the ball and my heart was thudding fast. The air around me seemed to crackle. I guessed, from the way Petra kicked it, that the ball would come straight at me and it would come high. I guessed right. I sprang to meet it, leaping up and pushing it away from me easily.

"Oh! Good save!" Petra complimented.

"No, it was rubbish," I said, chasing after the ball and throwing it back to her. "Go again."

"Why was that rubbish?" she asked. "You saved it!"

"Because I should have kept hold of it. Any waiting striker would have put that straight into the back of the net if it had been a real game."

"So? It's not a real game!" Petra called out.

"I know but… Just go again," I said. "Try to kick harder. And keep it low – that makes it more difficult for me." I'd watched enough games on TV with Dad to know that!

She did. She struck the ball harder and cleaner this time and I just managed to stick a leg in the way to deflect it.

"Nice one!" I said, returning the ball again.

"I'm just warming up!" she said. "I could score

every time but I don't want to show you up."

"In your dreams!"

Unfortunately most of Petra's shots were rubbish – either she hoofed them too far upwards and they landed miles away, or she tried too hard and they flew in the opposite direction. Sometimes she missed altogether, then slapped her forehead and said "D'oh!" like Homer Simpson.

Still, Petra never gives up, and the longer we played, the more determined she became, and she began planting a few past me. "Easy! Easy!" she chanted as she notched up number four.

6

**"You can always come off your line,"
a voice behind me said.**

I turned to see a lady looking at us. When I say
lady I mean she was older than a teenager but
miles younger than my mum. Maybe, like, twenty-
one or twenty-two?

The lady was wearing a navy blue tracksuit and
running on the spot. Her long light-brown hair was
tied back with a red bandana patterned with skulls.

"We're just practising," I said, in case she
thought we were messing about. She was kind
of official looking.

"So I see."

"I'm useless," Petra said.

"No, you're not. You just need to change a
few things. Look, I'll show you." The lady came

onto the pitch and held her hand out for the ball. "Watch."

She placed the ball on the ground and showed Petra, in slow motion, how to shoot using the front of her foot, not the toe the way Petra kept doing. The ball came straight to me, but not so hard I couldn't catch it.

"Your whole foot has to follow through," she instructed Petra. "You get more power to it then."

"Oh."

"You also need to make sure your entire body is balanced. Your arms, your head, your knees all have to be positioned correctly."

"All that just to kick a ball!"

"Yep!" The lady grinned, returning the ball to Petra.

"What's your name?" I asked as Petra began practising.

"Hannah."

"Before you go, will you take a penalty against me?" I asked, feeling a bit left out.

Hannah frowned. "But you're not wearing padded gear."

"Doesn't matter."

"It does!"

"Just one," I begged. "Please."

She shrugged, placed the ball on the spot, took a run up and kicked it straight at me. It was such a tame shot it barely reached me.

"No offence," I said, throwing it back to her, "but that was not your best attempt. I can tell."

Hannah chuckled. "OK."

This time she whacked it hard and low. I didn't even have time to think; I just stood there, stiff as a plank, as the ball thundered into the back of the net with a soft "thut".

"Well done," I said, rolling the ball back to her. "That was much better!"

"Thank you!" She laughed. "Right, I'd better be off."

I didn't want her to go. This was fun! "Just one more penalty? Please?"

"Sorry, love. I'm short of time."

"Please! Please! Please! Please! Please! Please!"

"Megan's what you call high-maintenance," Petra told her.

Hannah thought that was funny. She threw her head back and laughed out loud. It sounded lovely. "Go on, then," she said to me. "One more."

"Don't hold back just 'cos I'm a kid," I told her, "or a girl."

"Understood."

This time I crouched, my eye totally on the ball. I'd stop that shot going into my net if it killed me! My heart was thudding against my England shirt as the ball soared to my right, low but rising and heading straight for the back of the net. Without thinking I leapt, my right hand outstretched, my feet off the ground. It felt amazing, as if for a split second I were flying. The ball smacked against my palm and tilted over the crossbar before I crashed to the ground. I landed heavily, skinning my arm. Petra ran over and helped me up, but I was

laughing so much I didn't feel the pain. "I saved it."
I beamed at Hannah.

"You did" – she nodded – "but are you all right?"

"I feel brilliant."

"So you should! It was an excellent save – and
very brave."

"Your elbow's bleeding," Petra pointed out,
fumbling in her jeans pocket for a tissue.

"I saved it!" I said again, really chuffed with
myself. "I did a dive and I saved it."

Petra kept dabbing at my elbow and Hannah
began jogging again. "Good to see girls playing
football! Keep it up, both of you!" she called out,
waving to us as she headed towards the public
footpath that ran down the side of the ground.

The back of her tracksuit top had "Parrs" written
across it in big white letters.

We returned to Auntie Mandy's kitchen. As she
wiped gravel and dirt and blood from my arm, I sat
on the stool and stared into space. I must have

nodded yes and no to her when she asked me questions, but I wasn't really concentrating.

I was too distracted to talk. It isn't every day you discover what you want to be when you grow up. But I knew, from the minute Hannah struck that ball and I saved it, that I wanted to be a goalkeeper. Not just any goalkeeper, either. The England goalkeeper.

7

The next day I went straight to Mr Glasshouse. Forget fairy wings and tiaras; it was time for some straight talking.

"Mr Glasshouse," I said as he stood in the playground making sure everyone had heard the bell for morning registration.

He looked at me and smiled. It's easier to get his attention in the playground than on the field. He also seems more normal, more approachable, than when he's taking football practice. "Morning, Megan. Did you have a nice weekend?"

"I did, as it happens. I discovered what I want to do when I leave school."

"Really? That's..." He glanced over my shoulder and sighed. "Come on, Daisy! Come on, Dylan; the bell went five minutes ago!"

The McNeil twins in Year Two ran past. "Sorry, Mr Glasshouse! We overslept, then we wept and the mice crept!" they shouted in unison. The McNeil twins are weird.

"Anyway, Mr Glasshouse, I was wondering if you could help me out," I continued.

"Help you out?" he asked, looking a bit worried. "I'm a little busy, Megan… Can it wait until break? I'm taking assembly and then I've got to…"

I took a deep breath. My palms were sweating, but what I had to ask was too important to leave until break. "Thing is, I've decided I'm going to be goalie for England, so I wondered if you could put me straight into the school team. The sooner I start, the better."

"Excuse me?"

I took another deep breath and swallowed. "I wouldn't ask – I know I'm not in Year Six yet – but the thing is Michael Owen was only seven when he started. That's like, Year Two or Three. I'm way behind already."

"You want to go in goal for the school team?"

"Exactly." I gave him my best smile. I knew this was a big ask, especially as his son, Jack, was the current goalie.

Mr Glasshouse blinked a few times. "Well, all I can do is suggest you turn up for practices as you have been doing, Megan, and we'll see. You never know, perhaps next year…" He began to head inside.

I hurried after him. Once he'd taken assembly, he'd be in his office and that would be it. He'd be up to his armpits in paperwork. "No! Next year's too late, sir; I need to start now. I'm serious."

Mr Glasshouse stopped and looked at me intently.

I looked at him even more intently. I would not back down, even if my knees were shaking a little.

"Well, if you want to be goalkeeper for England – and why not? – wouldn't you be better practising keeping goal for a girls' team? It is the England Women you'd be playing for, after all."

I had to admit I hadn't thought of that. "Good point," I said.

He nodded and left.

I nodded and left.

It wasn't the result I'd hoped for, but it was better than nothing.

8

"I don't even know why I didn't think of it before," I said to Dad, flicking through the sports pages of the *Mowborough Mercury* later that night. "A girls only team. It's so obvious."

"Have you found one yet?" Dad asked.

I scowled. "No. I can't see anything about women's football in here. It's all men's or fishing or rugby."

"Try the Internet. There must be a league somewhere round here."

Dad was right. In our area there was the Nettie Honeyball Women's League. "What a funny name!" I said as I scrolled down the list of teams, clicking on one website after another, but every team I tried that had an Under 11s side was too far away. "Look at that one! The Grove Belles. They're top of the league *and* they've got junior squads!"

"Sorry, Megan." Dad sighed. "They're over in Ashtonby – it's twenty miles away. That just wouldn't work out when my shift overlapped with Mum's and you had a babysitter. You'd end up missing more matches than you attended."

I groaned inwardly. Why couldn't we live in a city like normal people? Manchester or Liverpool or London? Why did we have to live in boring old no-girls'-football-teams-for-miles Mowborough? "Oh, well. It was a nice dream while it lasted. Back to being an airline pilot," I said with a shrug.

Dad patted me on the shoulder as I switched the computer off. "It's a pity the Parrs don't have any junior teams," he said.

"What?"

"The Parrs. They're the women's team at Lornton FC."

"Oh!" I said. "The Parrs are a *team*. I thought that was Hannah's last name!" I explained about my encounter. "She's the one who inspired me!"

"Oh, I see. No, the 'Parrs' is the nickname of the women's team. They couldn't call themselves the Stags, like the men's team, so they chose Parrs. Not sure why. Look, why don't you phone Mandy now and ask her when they train. You can always go and watch."

Dads. Where would we be without them?

Auntie Mandy knew all about the Parrs. They trained at the ground every Tuesday from half-seven to half-nine. And guess what? Hannah – Hannah *Preston*, to give her full name – was the captain.

"Do you think they'd mind if I came to watch them train?"

"Course not. I'll come and watch with you; the bar's closed on Tuesday nights."

"Wicked!"

It was dark and drizzling when I arrived, so Auntie Mandy suggested we watch them practise from her living room instead. I pulled a chair as close to the window as I could and knelt on it. Auntie Mandy brought hot drinks for us – tea for her, hot chocolate with marshmallows for me – and together we watched the Parrs training on the floodlit pitch.

There were about twenty-five to thirty in the squad, like at my school. They jogged round the pitch in their tracksuits first, just like we did, then did stretches to warm up, just like we did. They even had a man shouting instructions at them, just like we did! Some of the drills were similar, too – the ones where you worked in small groups of three or four practising different types of passing.

It was interesting observing everything from a bird's-eye view. Well, I thought so, anyway. Auntie Mandy left after a few minutes to watch *Holby City*. I don't know how long I stayed there. I lost track of time.

Then someone blew a whistle and the players began clearing away all the cones and equipment. They were going to have a game! "Auntie Mandy, can I go and watch them outside?"

"As long as you wrap up warm and stay where I can see you!"

"Check!"

I dashed downstairs in time for the kick-off. It felt much better standing near the touchline – even if I was getting wet. The Parrs didn't seem to mind, so why should I? Their ponytails and fringes were dripping, their thin white shorts clinging to their legs. I pulled up the hood on my hoodie and watched, jumping up and down to keep warm.

One team was wearing blue bibs, the other yellow. My Parr – Hannah – was a blue and stood out in no time. She was the one who always seemed to find space. She was the one who chested the ball down once she'd received it, brought it instantly under control, turned, shielding her body over it like a crab so no one could take it off her, and then passed, all in one split second. She was the one who volleyed with the most accuracy. She was the one running, pointing, calling out to her team, spurring them on. She was The One, capital T capital O! I was so absorbed in watching her, remembering how nice she'd been to Petra and me, I almost forgot to watch the goalkeepers.

I focused on the one for the yellows, reckoning she'd see the most action. Unfortunately she was at the end furthest from me and I'd promised to stay where Auntie Mandy could see me, so it was difficult to get a great view of her catching and throwing and taking goal kicks. What I did see clearly was one of the yellow Parrs try to tackle Hannah on the halfway line, but she slipped and went over on her ankle. Play stopped, and all the bibs gathered round to help her up. It looked painful. When she tried to put her foot down, she winced and shook her head. She limped off and headed for the changing rooms. A sub came on and play resumed.

10

A minute later the yellows had a goal kick.
I had climbed onto the bench to watch how the
keeper would strike it in wet conditions when I was
distracted by a movement to my left. A girl about
my age came tearing out of the changing rooms,
heading straight towards me. Immediately the
injured Parrs player appeared hopping behind her.
"Oi! Come back here!" she yelled. "Stop her!"

I waited for someone to do something, but
nobody else seemed to have noticed; everyone was
concentrating on the game. The girl was so fast
I realized she'd fly past me any moment.

"Stop her!" the injured Parrs player called again.
"She's nicked our stuff!"

Without hesitation I jumped down from the bench,
then lunged at the girl as she drew parallel with me,

grabbing her sleeve and clinging to it. She spun round, taking me with her, and somehow we got tangled up in each other and both ended up with a thud on the wet tarmac. Even then she was twisting and turning, kicking out at me to get free. She landed a good, solid boot right on my knuckles so hard that I had to let go. Immediately she scrambled to her feet and disappeared along the footpath down the side of the clubhouse. I stood up, feeling shaken, sucking the back of my hand. It killed! She'd scraped all the skin off!

"Little monkey!" the Parrs player said when she reached me. "She was in the changing rooms going through all our stuff. I think I startled her. Mind you, she startled me, too! Are you all right?"

I nodded, trying not to cry. My hand was really stinging now and I felt wet and miserable.

"I'm Sian. What's your name?"

"Megan," I said.

"Megan, can you bend down and pick those things up for me? I'll fall over if I try!"

I nodded. On the ground were two mobiles, an iPod and a purse. I handed them over.

"Oh! That's my purse!" Sian gasped.

"Glad you got it back."

"Honestly, you can't turn your back for one second... But thanks again. You were a star. Do you live round here?"

"No, but my Auntie Mandy is the manager of the clubhouse."

"Oh, right. OK. Well, you'd better let her clean that hand up for you – it looks sore."

I nodded and returned to Auntie Mandy's flat. What a rubbish way to end the night!

Auntie Mandy was upset when she saw me. My clothes were wet and muddy and I was shaking all over. I had post-*dra*matic stress! She made me stand in front of the gas fire while she bathed my hand.

"The girl was about my age." I sniffed. "With long dark hair."

"I bet I know who it was. Jenny-Jane Bayliss! She

lives across the road. She hovers outside sometimes and asks for jobs. I used to feel sorry for her, but she'll be getting no more sympathy from me—"

Auntie Mandy was cut off mid-sentence by the sound of someone calling up the stairs.

"What now? Hang on a tick, Megan," she said.

A minute later she was back with Hannah Preston and the yellows' goalie. They were both wearing their tracksuits and had ruffled hair, as if they'd just dried it quickly with a towel. "Hannah and Katie wanted a word, Megan," said Auntie Mandy.

"Hi, Megan! Are you OK?" Hannah Preston asked. Her voice was full of concern.

I stared at her, a bit overwhelmed at seeing her again.

She waved her mobile phone. "I just wanted to say thank you. Sian says you retrieved this for me. I'm so grateful! I'd be totally lost without it!"

"That's OK," I mumbled.

"And that was my iPod she took, the little minx!" Katie added.

"I think I know who she is," Auntie Mandy said. "I'll be having words in the morning."

Hannah cocked her head to one side. "Have I seen you before, Megan?" Her eyes lit up before I could answer. "I know you! You're the kamikaze goalie!"

I grinned. "That's me!"

She turned to Katie. "Do you remember me telling you about when I was jogging on Sunday and came across the two little girls playing? This was the cheeky one who made me take my penalty kick again!"

"You were being easy on me!" I said.

She laughed that same lovely laugh from before. "Well, I owe you! If there's anything I can do, just let me know."

My heart was already thumping from what had just happened, but when she said that it clattered like a fire bell. "Are you sure?" I asked, a grin on my face wider than Wembley Stadium.

11

**Hannah looked a bit stunned for
a moment after I'd asked her.** "Coach you?
Oh, I don't know about that… I am halfway through
the Level One Coaching course, but…"

Luckily Katie backed me up. "Don't be mean,
Han; the girl deserves a reward! I'll help. She wants
to be a goalkeeper, after all, and the most important
player on the team needs all the advice she can
get!" Katie winked at me. From that moment on
I liked her almost as much as I liked Hannah.

"Go on, then!" Hannah said. "Drop down here at
half-six for half an hour before practice on Tuesdays
– if that's OK with you, Mandy?"

"Absolutely fine by me!"

"Which team do you play for?" Katie asked me.

"I don't. I train with my school team, but I don't

exactly play for them…" I felt my chin wobble. "I've been looking for a girls' team and the Grove Belles looked good, but…"

Hannah and Katie spluttered. "Grove Belles! Don't mention those cheating hyenas in front of us!"

"Big rivals," Auntie Mandy informed me in a loud whisper.

Katie scowled. "They're big somethings! You mustn't go to them, Megan! Promise us!"

"I promise."

"How many others are there like you at school, Megan? Little girls who want to play but don't get a chance?" asked Hannah.

"I don't know exactly. A few, I suppose." I rattled off some names.

Katie grabbed Hannah's arm. "Are you thinking what I'm thinking?"

Hannah frowned. "I don't think so," she said slowly.

"Yes you are! Let's do it! Let's start a team up.

It'll be cool. Like Little Ant and Little Dec. We'll have Little Parrs!"

"Parrs' Nips!" Hannah laughed.

"Parsnips?" I said.

Hannah stared thoughtfully at her mobile, then looked up and grinned. "OK, you've twisted my arm!" she said. "If the club gives permission, bring your friends, too, to practise."

"Really?"

"Really. A training only basis, mind."

"Oh," I said, my face dropping.

"What's the matter?" Katie asked.

"Well… No offence, but some of the girls I'm thinking of – the skilled ones – go to training already. They probably won't come if they don't get to play real matches; not for half an hour. I mean, *I'll* come, definitely, but *they* might not…" I trailed off. I felt awful now for sounding ungrateful, but it was the truth.

Hannah nodded. "I can see where you're coming from, Megan, but getting a real team up and running is a lot of hard work. You have to register and get sponsors…"

"Not to mention money for the kit and everything," Katie added.

"Oh," I said.

"We've made her all sad again now!" Katie laughed.

Hannah glanced down at me. "Tell you what: if the girls who come have the right attitude and show real potential, we'll look into forming a proper league team. I'm not saying Katie and I will run it or anything, but we'll look into it and do all we can to help. And we'll start at six so you get a full hour. How does that sound?"

"It sounds…" I gulped and looked at both the Parrs players, hoping they wouldn't notice my eyes filling with tears. "It sounds awesome!"

Auntie Mandy clapped her hands together in delight. "Oh, how wonderful!"

12

The next morning I took my England notepad and pencil with me to school and set about recruiting straight away. I began on Nightingale table during Literacy Hour. "Petra, I know you're not that bothered about football but you are my best friend, so if you'd like to come…"

Instead of answering she stared at my hand. "What happened? Has Whiskas been scratching you?"

My knuckles were still red and sore from where Jenny-Jane had crunched them. "Yes," I said, thinking that blaming my poor cat was better than explaining about Jenny-Jane. "Now … about this football training with that lady you met. In or out?"

"In, of course!" she said. "Especially Tuesdays. Charlotte has a riding lesson and telly's rubbish."

"Excellento!"

The other three on my table were boys, so I couldn't ask them. I glanced round to check where Miss Parkinson, my crabby form teacher, was, thinking I might risk a trip across to Einstein table, when Yuri Kozak, who sat opposite me, leaned forward. "Put name on list," he said.

"It's just for girls!" I whispered. Yuri is from the Ukraine. He's only been at Mowborough for a few weeks and his English isn't so good yet. I pulled my hair to show what I meant. "Girls!" I repeated.

"I know! Put sister down. In next class. She is good football. Play in old school!"

"Oh!" I said. "Cool! What's her name?"

"Nika."

"Is that you talking, Megan Fawcett?" Miss Parkinson asked. She must have bat's ears. She's certainly got a bat's face.

At lunchtime, Petra had clarinet so I searched round for Tabinda, who agreed instantly to come on the team. "Girls only! Neat!"

I asked her to help me recruit more players. Obviously we started on the playing field. Our playing field is divided into two: the wood end (two trees and a bench), where the little ones go, and the car-park end, where the older ones go. "Right, you do Wood End and I'll do this end. Meet you back here in ten minutes."

"Right-oh."

I watched as Tabinda ran to the far side of the field, then I took a deep breath and looked around. I spotted two of the Year Six girls who were on the school team but, to be honest, they looked a bit scary. I don't know what Year Sixes eat but it makes them taller than boys and laugh too loud. Then I had a brain wave. Don't ask the ones already on the team, my brain said, in waves; ask the ones who are like you. The ones trying to get on the team. They'll be more up for it! I am such a genius sometimes.

Switching direction, I strode over to the painted tractor tyre where the Year Fours hang out. Year Four girls are much less frightening than Year Sixes.

Nika, Yuri's sister, was there, sandwiched between Eve Akboh and Lucy Skidmore. How convenient! I already knew Eve a little because her mum is a nurse at Mowborough General, like mine. Better still, Eve and Lucy both go to Mr Glasshouse's football practice too!

"A girls' football team?" Lucy asked. "Sounds good. What time's practice?"

"Six o'clock on Tuesdays."

"Can we be in both footy teams?" Eve asked.

"Course."

They shrugged. "Let's go for it!"

"Will you explain all this to Nika? Her brother told me she used to play at her old school."

"Did she? We never knew that!" Lucy said.

They set about miming football shapes and kicking while I wrote their names down on my England pad. Nika seemed eager and spelled out her last name – Kozak – for me to add to my list.

"OK. I'll be in touch when I have more details," I said.

"Hey, Megan," Eve called as I turned away.

"Yes?"

"There are two girls at the after-school club who might be interested. Amy Minter and Gemma Hurst. They don't go to this school, though."

"That's not a problem," I said quickly.

"I'll check with them tonight."

"Wicked," I said, scribbling down the extra names. This was turning out better than I'd expected.

Tabinda only had two names: Daisy and Dylan McNeil.

"What?" I asked. "Please tell me you're kidding!"

"Look, Megan, I know they are only in Year Two and a little bit psycho …"

"A little?"

"… but they are keen. And fast. They can outrun Mr Glasshouse and all the lunchtime supervisors; I've seen them."

I thought for a moment. At school the team was seven-a-side, but the Parrs played eleven-a-side so maybe the Parsnips would, too. Even if they didn't we'd need enough players to have games against each other. Ten or twelve at least. "OK," I said, adding the twins to my list. "Thanks, Tabinda."

She squeezed my arm. "It's going to be great. Like that film – *Bend It Like Beckham*!"

"Only better!"

She dashed off, her plaits bouncing up and down her back as she ran.

I went to meet Petra in the dining room for second sitting. She had saved me a place with her clarinet case and moved it when I arrived.

"Good news – I've got ten names already," I said.

"Minty." She opened her sandwich box and began arranging her lunch in a line, savoury to sweet. She always does this. It's weird, but not as weird as the McNeil twins who were heading our way.

They arrived with a whoosh, clambering over chairs and sitting either side of me. Don't ask me which one was Daisy and which one was Dylan because I don't know. They both have the same blonde hair cut to chin level. They both have the same blue eyes and sticky-out ears. They both have the same annoying laugh, like a donkey stuck in a lift. "Meganini! Thanks for letting us join Girls FC!" said the twin on my left.

"It's the one for me!" said the one on my right.

"It's where we want to be."

"Playing for girls, you see."

"Not UC, FC."

The twins cracked up. Luckily, Mrs Woolcock, who used to be Miss Barnes until a few weeks ago when she got married, was supervising the next table. "Keep the noise down, girls, please," she said.

"Sorry!" they chimed. "We're just excited about playing football on Megan's girls' team. We're going now. Smell you later!" They sprang out of their seats and tiptoed out of the dining hall making *shh!* noises.

Mrs Woolcock looked at me. "Really? A girls' football team? That's a good idea."

"Thanks," I said.

"Is it only open to girls at this school? I'm sure Holly would love to join, but she goes to Saddlebridge Primary."

"Holly?"

"My stepdaughter. She's very keen – well … she goes to watch Leicester City with her father. I'm sure she'd love to play and she could do with the exercise."

"I'll put her down," I said, scrambling around for my pad.

"Do," Mrs Woolcock said, then she bit her bottom lip and looked worried.

"Is something wrong?" I asked.

"No … just … please don't tell her what I said about her needing exercise… She's a bit sensitive about her weight."

"We won't," Petra promised.

After I had added Holly's name I recited my list to Petra. "So that's me, you, Tabinda, Nika, Lucy, Eve, Amy, Gemma, Daisy, Dylan and Holly. Yay! I've got eleven! I've got a full team! Maybe more!"

13

I was so nervous that first practice! Much worse than usual, when I feel sick and shaky and have to take deep breaths before going out on the field. This time I kept doing "What if?" questions in my head. What if Hannah and Katie changed their minds? What if the committee wouldn't let us play? What if nobody turned up? What if they turned up and Hannah and Katie thought we were all rubbish and wasting their time? What if the field caught fire? What if *I* caught fire?

Of course none of that happened. Everyone turned up. The committee said they'd be happy to let us train for an hour, provided all the parents signed consent forms saying they wouldn't blame them if their daughters broke something/were hit by lightning/got attacked by trolls at half-time or any of those other things grown-ups worry about.

The only slightly weird thing that happened was that instead of eleven players we had twelve. Auntie Mandy had invited that Jenny-Jane Bayliss along too. Yes, I'm serious!

When she had told me on the phone the night before, I couldn't believe my ears. I looked from the receiver to my knuckles and back again. Auntie Mandy said she knew it was a strange thing to do, but explained that when she went round to Jenny-Jane's house it was so obvious why Jenny-Jane behaved the way she did that she didn't have the heart to take things further.

"Huh!" I grunted.

Auntie Mandy could tell I was a bit miffed. "Everyone deserves a second chance, don't they, Megan?"

"I suppose," I replied.

"Besides," Auntie Mandy said, "if Jenny-Jane is playing football with you, she can't be pinching purses and iPods, can she?"

"I guess not."

"And Hannah agreed."

"Did she?"

"She said if I vouched for Jenny-Jane, then it was OK with her."

"Well, if it's OK with Hannah, it's OK with me," I said.

So there were twelve of us gathered on the field that evening. While I waited for Hannah and Katie to start, I couldn't help giving Jenny-Jane a few sidelong glances. I was worried she might give me a sneery look as if to show she'd got one over on me, but she never so much as peered at me once. Instead I noticed that her trainers were dirty and scuffed and her joggers were a bit short for her legs. She looked pale and on edge and I suddenly felt sorry for her. I thought about what Auntie Mandy had said about everyone deserving a second chance. When Petra asked who Jenny-Jane was

I just shrugged and said, "Someone from the village," which was true.

Then Hannah and Katie stepped forward and introduced themselves. "Welcome to Lornton FC, girls." Hannah grinned, and I forgot all about Jenny-Jane and all about feeling nervous. It was time to get down to business!

14

I loved those early sessions; they were awesome. After getting us to jog round the pitch and then showing us how to do proper stretches to warm up our muscles, Hannah took us through all sorts of exercises and drills to improve our co-ordination and agility. As well as using cones, she borrowed these things called fast foot ladders from the senior team. These were used to teach us different running and jumping techniques. They were great fun!

After that we worked in pairs, doing simple stuff like tapping the ball back and forth gently to each other, using different parts of the foot. It might sound basic but it's not as easy as it looks when you're a beginner! I always started with Petra, and she kept kicking it too hard and I kept not kicking it hard enough so we ended up either having to run for the ball or walking to it to start again! Then we swapped partners and practised something else. This way, we all got to know each other. I suppose we could tell what stage we were at, too.

Nika was good, just like her brother said she would be, and you could tell Eve and Lucy had played before. Eve's friend Gemma was really skilled, too – better than Eve, actually. Holly, Mrs Woolcock's stepdaughter, was a bit on the chubby side like Mrs Woolcock had implied but she joined in, no problem, and always kept up. Jenny-Jane was quiet and didn't mix much but she was nippy on the ball. The only trouble was that once she had it she wouldn't let go. "Hoggy Bayliss" I called her. I didn't really mind, though. At least she tried. So did the twins, amazingly. They were usually the last to arrive and needed Hannah to repeat things to them about twenty times, but their enthusiasm was real enough.

The only one I didn't like much was Amy Minter, Eve's other friend from after-school club. I don't know why Amy came. She was one of those girlie-girls who wear too much pink. Even her trainers were pink! During training, Amy would do some of the drills but whenever she got a bit bored she'd mess about or do silly things to get attention, like knocking all the cones out of the way or picking the ball up and running with it. It did my head in. I was worried Hannah and Katie wouldn't go through with forming the team if Amy carried on being silly.

The best bit of every training session was towards the end of the hour. "OK, who's ready for a game?" Hannah would ask.

We'd all cheer. Let's face it, a game was what we'd been waiting for. It was usually six-a-side. "Line up then," Hannah would tell us, a bundle of blue bibs in her arm for one team, yellow over the other arm for the opposing team. "And remember, no tackling until I've taught you how. I don't want any injuries. Just close marking, please."

We probably looked rubbish to anyone watching at that time. Everyone would soon forget their positions and we'd be running all over the place like wild ponies. I'd be in goal, watching it all unfold. Sometimes my whole defence would go AWOL, leaving me with the opposition charging at me, and I'd feel outnumbered like the soldiers in *Zulu* (my dad's favourite film). Except I wasn't scared; it was too immense, too exciting to be scary. Those training sessions were the highlight of my week.

15

I think it was in late April, maybe our fifth or sixth week of training, when things changed. I knew Katie wouldn't be there because she'd told us she had to work overtime that Tuesday, and I remember having a bit of a cold, but apart from that everything should have been normal – but when I arrived at the ground I saw both fields being used. The Lornton Stags were playing a league game on the main pitch, and the training pitch was set up for training: all the equipment was out – but so were about twenty boys, running in and out of the cone channels, stepping in and out of the fast foot ladders ... all the stuff we did.

I walked over to the touchline. "What's happening?" I asked Tabinda.

She shrugged. "Looks like someone's using our pitch."

"Maybe they're just finishing off," I suggested.

"I don't think so. Not if that's anything to go by." She nodded towards the far side of the pitch.

I glanced across to where Hannah and a man in a tracksuit were having a bit of an argument. Hannah kept pointing to her watch, then pointing at us. The guy – I didn't know who he was – just shrugged.

More of the girls arrived and eventually Hannah walked over, her face apologetic. "I'm sorry," she said, "there's been some sort of … mix up. We can't train tonight."

"But it's *our* time," Lucy said.

"I know!" Hannah agreed, glaring angrily at the man, who was bellowing something at one of the boys. "But as we're not a 'proper' team, we don't have priority."

"That's not fair," Tabinda said.

"So we've got to go home without even touching a ball?" Eve asked. "That sucks!"

"Can't we *share* the pitch?" I asked. "Have half each?"

Hannah shook her head. "I suggested that already. I was turned down flat."

"This is so annoying! I'm missing *America's Top Model* to come here," Amy grumbled, with a flick of her hair.

Hannah sighed. "Look, I know it's annoying, but there's nothing I can do. Have you all got phones to call home? Otherwise you can use mine."

"Who is he, anyway?" I asked, glancing across.

"Gary Browne. He's the manager of the Under 10s."

"Oh." I frowned. I was sure I'd heard Auntie Mandy talking about one of the managers being a miserable old coot. I wondered if she meant him.

A second later I had my answer. Dylan and Daisy had begun running up and down, pretending to be aeroplanes bombing each other. Dylan (I had learned to tell the difference between them now – Dylan was always sucking a strand of her hair, Daisy wasn't) accidentally clattered into one of the cones, catching Gary Browne's attention. He shouted something, but Hannah, calling one of our mums on her mobile, had her back to him and didn't hear. He jogged towards us.

Up close Gary Browne was quite scary: short but broad-shouldered, with thin hair brushed back from his leathery face. His mouth was set in a hard line. "What's going on here?" he demanded, coming to a halt just in front of us. "Hannah – move these little girls, will you? They're putting my lads off!"

"Zoooooooooooooom!" said Dylan, swerving round him.

Hannah turned and switched off her phone. "Oh, OK, sorry," she said. "Come on, you lot; let's go and watch the other match. We'll be able to pick up some tips."

"Huh! I doubt it," the creep Gary Browne muttered.

Hannah stopped in her tracks. "Meaning?" she asked.

The coach's eyes narrowed. "Oh, it's more than

my job's worth to say, isn't it? I'll be accused of all sorts!" His eyes swept over us dismissively. It was so obvious what he was thinking: girls shouldn't be allowed near a football pitch. I felt my cheeks burn with anger.

He began to head off, but as he turned I grabbed his sleeve and pulled it hard. He turned back and scowled at me. "What are you doing?" he asked.

I wasn't sure myself. All I knew was that I was really cross. My heart was racing, but I kept hold of his jumper. "Give us a match," I said.

"What?"

"Ten minutes each way."

"Don't be ridiculous. And let go of my sleeve, please."

Next to me, Daisy and Dylan took up the chant. "Ten minutes! Ten minutes!"

"What's the matter? Are you worried we'll beat you?" I challenged.

Everyone was chanting now, "Ten minutes, ten minutes." It was a bit off-putting but I didn't dare back down. A Fawcett always finishes what she's started. Unfortunately.

Gary Browne focused on me. He tried to control his face and gave me a Miss Parkinson-type smile – you know, totally fake and more scary than a vampire at sunset. "Look, petal, I know what'll happen. One of my lads'll tackle you and you'll be crying your eyes out and screaming blue murder! I don't want that responsibility."

"Try us!"

"Megan," Hannah said, "Gary's right. You're not ready yet."

"Play mixed sides, then, like in school!"

"No! Not going to happen! Not in a million years!" the boys' coach grunted, shrugging my hand away.

"Yellow! Yellow! Yellow!" Amy and Eve now chanted.

Gary Browne did not like that. "Yellow? Don't make me laugh!"

"Yellow! Yellow! Yellow!" they continued.

Gary Browne's face stiffened with anger. "Right.

If that's what you want," he said briskly, in the fastest changing of a mind I've ever known. "Five minutes each way, seven-a-side. Hurry up; some of us have got a *proper* match to prepare for."

"Fine," I agreed.

"Make sure you warm up properly!"

"You heard the man!" I said and led us in a trot round the outer edge of the field.

"Megan!" Hannah said, coming up alongside me.

"Yes, coach," I said, glancing at her nervously out of the corner of my eye. I had disobeyed her. I had got us a match against who-knows-what kind of opposition.

"I like your style," she said and veered off.

16

Once we were warmed up, Hannah gathered us in a circle. "Look, you know you're not going to win or anything daft like that, don't you? This team are near the top of their league."

We nodded. We knew.

"So all you can do is try your best. Remember everything you've done in training. Have you all got shin pads on?"

We nodded. We had.

"OK, positions… Based on what I've seen the past few weeks …"

My heart thudded. I was always in goal when we played our six-a-sides – but so was Amy Minter for the opposite side. What if I didn't get picked? I'd be devastated!

"… Tabz, let's have you up front to start, with

Nika, Gemma and JJ in midfield. Er … Holly in defence with Lucy. And Meggo…" I looked at her. I think I almost stopped breathing.

She grinned. "I guess you're in goal."

"Yes, coach!"

"Get yourself some gloves from the storeroom."

Yes! Yes! Yes!

Amy's face crumpled. "Where do I go?"

"On the bench for the first half."

"That's not fair. I've been in goal as much as Megan has!"

Hannah sighed. "I know! You can swap round at half-time, OK?"

"Huh," Amy muttered.

We kicked off. Five minutes doesn't sound like a long time, does it? It wasn't long enough for me to get nervous like I usually do, but it was long enough for me to let in four goals. Yep. Four.

The first one caught me out before I'd had time to think – a clear, clean shot from their number 9.

The second one, a minute later, was more scrappy. I totally lost sight of the ball because there were so many bodies around me – mostly my team, it has to be said – and their player, a tall kid with gelled-up blond hair, just tapped it in after it had rebounded off Holly's knee. He had the cheek to smirk at me, too. I didn't blame him. I didn't have a clue what I was doing, to be honest.

Their third goal was a brilliant header from a corner. I was watching the ball all the way, moving back, back, all the time. It came in high. I leapt, thinking, this one's mine! I almost got to it with my fingertips, but a dark head made contact with the ball first and nodded it straight into the back of the net, taking me with it. The fact that the dark head belonged to Lucy didn't help. "I'm so sorry," she said, helping me up. She had tears in her eyes. "I'm so sorry!"

"Hey," I said, smiling at her as I brushed myself down, "it still beats netball, right?"

The fourth one was a penalty. Jenny-Jane

decided the easiest way to stop the number 9 who kept outpacing her was to trip him up. She wasn't even subtle about it. "He dived!" she protested.

Gary Browne blew the whistle and pointed to the spot.

It was the best part of the match. My first time facing a real penalty! Argh!

The tall kid with the gelled-up hair placed the ball on the penalty spot. He looked at me, grinned, pulled up his left sock, then his right, then his left again.

I crouched, waiting, waiting. I knew from watching *Match of the Day* that I mustn't move yet or he'd know which way I was going to dive. I watched as he ran up. He swung with his right leg, kicking the ball with the inside of his foot. Left! It's going left, my brain yelled. I dived left – and chose correctly, but there was such a swerve on the ball that it curled away from me and I crashed to the ground empty-handed.

Four–nil!

The boy came up to return the ball to the centre spot. "Good try," he said.

"Yeah, sure."

"It was. You moved in the right direction."

Big deal, I thought – but at least he was being friendly.

In fact, all the boys were all right. None of them tried to foul us or made fun or anything; they just played. It was only their horrible coach who kept spoiling things, barking at them constantly. "Mark up, Kieron! Mark up! Sloppy, Jack! Sloppy! What was that supposed to be, Scott, you dozy waste of space?" I felt sorry for them, having to put up with him all the time.

So we went into the second half four–nil down. We had a two-minute break for team tactics before we were to begin again. "Well played! Well played!" Hannah told us. "I'm so proud of you all!"

I went to hand Amy the gloves. "I'm not wearing those," she said. "They'll be all sweaty. I've got these from my mum's shop." She pulled out a pair of jazzy stripy yellow-and-orange knitted ones.

"Please yourself," I said, not looking at her.

I walked over to Petra and she gave me a hug. "You are so brave! You almost saved that penalty! I had my fingers, toes and eyes crossed for you."

"So did I! That's why I missed!" I joked.

Hannah made several more changes so that everyone had a go. Petra swapped with Holly, Daisy with Lucy, Dylan with Jenny-Jane, Tabinda with Eve. Only Nika and Gemma stayed put. Hannah also made Amy wear the proper gloves. Amy wasn't impressed!

It was our kick-off. Gemma, in the centre circle, passed to Petra, and Petra tried dribbling the ball forward – but she kicked it too far and their number 6 swooped. He nipped it away and crossed it to his right wing. The winger mis-kicked it, though – I think it was Scott, the one Gary Browne had called a dozy waste of space – and it landed at Nika's feet.

She took the ball back into their half, then looked up, but there was no one to pass to so she ran further upfield. By now she had two of their players chasing her down. "Man on!" I warned. My heart was racing so much! Nika spurted forward again. It was the most we'd held possession all match. She looked round again and just walloped the ball into the penalty area. It was beautiful, arcing like an invisible rainbow.

Somehow the ball landed right in front of an unmarked Gemma, who immediately chested it down as if she'd being doing it all her life, then swung her left foot and whacked it towards the goal. The goalie leapt and punched it out – but only as far as Eve, who headed it straight back at him. *Headed it!* We hadn't even practised those! But the blooming goalie got an arm to it again and that was that. He threw it out towards one of his midfielders, who darted away with it. I don't think the ball left our half again.

The boys were just too experienced. They scored

three more times and hit the woodwork twice, but I was still sad when the whistle for full time went. Not only because I was enjoying the game so much, but also – and I know this sounds awful – because if we'd had longer they'd have scored more. Three in the second half meant Amy had a better record than I did. Yes, I know that's not the right attitude. I'm only human!

What was nice was that the boys clapped us off. Gelled-up hair shouted, "Three cheers for the girls!" and the team cheered.

I realized our team didn't know what to do. We were all staring at each other, wondering if the boys were taking the mickey. "Three cheers for Lornton!" I shouted, walking back onto the pitch and leading the applause.

I even went up to Gary Browne and shook his hand and thanked him for reffing. "You're welcome," he said gruffly, then blew his whistle again. "Right, lads," he shouted, "now that's over let's get down to some serious business."

We all felt a bit deflated then. None of our parents had arrived yet and we were all really hyper after the short game. "I know!" I said. "I'll go and ask Auntie Mandy to open the bar for us!" I dashed off.

17

I don't think the clubhouse had ever heard such a racket. Honestly, you'd have thought we'd won the Premiership! It was all "Did you see...?" and "I tried to kick, but..." and "What about when..."

Auntie Mandy just stood there, a bemused look on her face.

"We've just played the Under 10s," I told her. "We got whupped!"

"I see." She laughed, running water into a big jug of concentrated orange-and-pineapple squash and putting it on the bar for us.

I was about to go into detail when Hannah blew her whistle and I scuttled across to where Petra was holding a space for me. I squished in between her and Nika.

"Listen up, gang," Hannah said. Her eyes had a glint in them. "I am so made up with every one of you! That took guts, taking on an experienced side like that. Lily Parr would have been dead proud of you."

"Lily who?" Eve asked.

"Lily Parr. The player the Parrs are nicknamed after. Haven't I told you about her?"

"No!" we chorused.

"Well, I should have!" Hannah said. "She was a legend. She played for a team called Dick, Kerr's Ladies about ... oh, it must be over ninety years ago now."

"There were women's teams then?" I asked.

"Dead right there were! Getting crowds of over fifty thousand, too. Lily Parr was famous. She scored over forty-three goals in her first season and she was only fourteen. She's in the English Football Hall of Fame."

"Go Lily!" Daisy shouted.

"Before her there was Nettie Honeyball. That's

who the Nettie Honeyball Women's League is named after."

We shook our heads.

"Never heard of her? Well, look her up too! While you're at it, look up players like Rachel Yankey and Kelly Smith, who've played for England recently. Or Mia Hamm, the American player. Or go and watch top sides like Arsenal Ladies or Everton. You'll see how brilliantly women can play together in a team."

"Could we ever be that good? Like Arsenal?" Tabinda asked.

"I don't see why not, if you work at it," Hannah said.

"We'd need to be in a league first, wouldn't we?" Lucy asked. "To play other teams?"

"Yes," Hannah said slowly, "and I think you could do really well, but setting up a team from scratch is all sorts of hassle – you have to register and get insurance and have money for this and money for that…"

As Hannah gave the same reasons she'd given

me weeks before, my head dropped. So there wouldn't be a team after all. Not a *real* team, with a kit and fixtures and rivals and minibus outings to away games. I bit back my disappointment. Oh well. Training with Hannah and Katie was still better than football practice with Mr Glasshouse. At least I got individual attention from them. Plus I liked playing with just girls. I liked being a goalie. That wouldn't happen at school. I took a deep breath, lifted my head and smiled. Putting on a brave face, my mum calls it.

Then Auntie Mandy spoke. "Do you mind if I ask something, Hannah?"

"Shoot," Hannah replied.

"Are you saying it's only a matter of money to get a girls' team going? Once you've cleared all the legal stuff?"

"Basically."

"And you'd continue to coach them?"

"Definitely. I've enjoyed it more than I thought I would! So has Katie."

Auntie Mandy turned to us. "And are you girls all serious? I mean, I know our Megan is, but the rest of you?"

At that we nearly blew the roof off the clubhouse!

Auntie Mandy had to put her hands over her ears to drown out the yells. "All right! All right! I get the message! Well, if that's all, I'll start the fundraising right here, right now." She told me to go round to the kitchen and grab the largest empty jar I could find. Two minutes later I was back with a gherkin jar as big as a goldfish bowl. Auntie Mandy produced a sticky white label and a felt pen from a drawer next to the till. "The Parrs Under 11s fund. Please give generously," she wrote. She stuck the label across the front of the jar and placed it in the centre of the bar. "That stays there until it's full," she declared. "Then the money gets banked and we start again until you've got enough."

"Lovely jubbly!" someone called out.

You can rearrange this well-known footballing phrase to describe how I felt: moon the over.

☆ ☆ ☆

The mums and dads didn't know what had hit them when they arrived to pick everyone up. Talk about hyper! I was glad Auntie Mandy was taking me home; if mum had walked through the door I'd probably have squashed her flat.

"Wow!" Hannah said as the last parents waved goodbye. "That was something!"

"Awesome," I told her, "the word is awesome!"

18

I expect you think I'm going to bang on about how we had to do loads of daft things to raise money, like sitting in baths of baked beans and running cake stalls and selling raffle tickets to guess the name of a panda with half its stuffing missing. Well, actually, we never had to do any of that stuff, which is a shame in a way as I quite like the idea of sitting in a bath of baked beans.

Basically, all the parents and guardians thought that their girls playing football in a proper team and eventually in a proper league was a great thing to support. Tabinda's dad, who runs a garden centre just outside Mowborough, sponsored us and provided the home and away kit. (The downside of that is the garden centre is called Sweet Peas and that's what is written on the front of our shirts. No offence, Mr Shah, and I don't want to sound ungrateful, but I'd rather be called a parsnip than a sweet pea.)

Loads of other parents volunteered to do other stuff – organizing transport to away matches, sorting out membership and subs and publicity. Within a month we had all bases covered. All we had to do now was turn up!

Here's what it said about us in the Parrs' newsletter:

LORNTON FC
Parrs News Latest
Parrs Under 11s

On 27 April we were delighted to welcome a new squad to the club: the Parrs Under 11s (the Parsnips).

Originally, the girls came to Lornton FC's ground simply to enjoy training sessions run by

Parrs captain Hannah Preston. It soon became obvious that these youngsters wanted and deserved match practice, and with the massive support of their parents and Mandy Leggitt, at the clubhouse, enough capital was raised to form a squad.

Says Hannah: "I was overwhelmed by how enthusiastic the girls were. All of them have such a positive attitude to the game I had no hesitation in agreeing to coach them as a proper team."

The girls will play in the Parrs colours of red shirt with white sleeves, white shorts and red socks with white trim. The home and away strip has been sponsored by Mr and Mrs R. Shah of Sweet Peas Garden Centre, Mowborough Road, Mowborough.

THE PARRS UNDER 11S

Megan Fawcett, Petra Ward, Lucy Skidmore, Dylan McNeil, Holly Woolcock, Nika Kozak, Jenny-Jane Bayliss, Gemma Hurst, Eve Akboh, Tabinda Shah, Daisy McNeil and Amy Minter

COACH: Hannah Preston
ASSISTANT COACH: Katie Regan

There was even a team photo of all of us. Well, nearly all – Gemma was away that day. Eve told me she missed training on purpose because she hates having her photo taken. "Weird, isn't it? You'd think with her background she'd be used to it," Eve said. I asked her what she meant but she just chewed her lip and looked uncomfortable. "Oh, nothing. Forget it."

So I did, until much later but that's another story!

One day at the start of May, Hannah waited until training had finished and then took us to the changing rooms. Usually we all turned up in our gear and went home in the same gear, so we'd never been in the changing rooms before. "I just wanted to show you in here," Hannah said. "This is where you'll get changed before matches and where I'll talk to you about tactics." She pushed open the door.

"Don't get excited," Katie warned us. "They need a bit of a makeover."

A bit! I was well disappointed. It was just a cold,

rectangular room with lockers and slatted benches round the sides and two showers at one end with chipped white tiles. The place smelled of damp and disinfectant.

But none of that mattered really, because in the middle of the floor were two huge cartons tied with red and white ribbons that Tabinda's dad had left there earlier. Even Tabinda was surprised. "He never told me!" she gushed.

We all got over-excited and started pulling at the ribbons, so Hannah made us sit on the benches while Katie dished out the kits, still in their plastic bags. Shirts, shorts, then socks. The bags kept sliding off everyone's knees. It was great fun – until Katie got to the goalkeeper's spot. There was only the one. It was a dark green and black padded top. Amy grabbed it out of Katie's hand before I could say anything. I felt my eyes sting with tears. I couldn't help it. What if Hannah let Amy have the keeper's kit? After all, she had let in fewer goals than me that time against the boys' team.

"Why isn't it red like the others?" Amy asked,
a scowl on her face as deep as a gorge.

"The goalie has to stand out from the rest of the
team," Katie explained.

"Well, I'm not wearing that! I want to wear red.
Green is not a good colour for me!"

"Is she sure about that?" Petra muttered next
to me. "I think green sums her up pretty neatly!"

Katie must have thought the same. "Just as well,
then," she told Amy, and she plucked the kit out of
her hand and threw it to me. "For you, Meggo!"
she said. "Never a doubt."

One of the tears rolled down my cheek before
I could stop it. I'm such a big baby!

"She's welcome to it," Amy sneered and started
foraging for her size in the remaining red and
white kits.

So that was that. I was the Parrs Under 11s
number 1. I'd made it this far. I sat there, just staring
at the padded top, thinking it was the most beautiful
thing I'd ever held in my life.

"OK, ladies, stop rustling. I've got more news," Hannah told us. She delved into her bag and pulled out an envelope. "This came today. We have been officially accepted into the Nettie Honeyball Women's League!"

We looked at each other, our faces what my nan would call "a picture". Someone gasped; actually I think it was me.

"We've got such a wide age range among us I've had to put us in the Under 11s. We're one of two new teams. The other one is called Southfields Athletic – making ten teams in the league altogether. I'll let you have a fixture list as soon as possible."

There was a bit of a commotion involving high fives, stomping and a mini Mexican wave.

"Hang on, hang on. There's more!" Hannah laughed. "Because the new season doesn't kick off until September and you need some match experience before then, Southfields Athletic wondered if we'd like a friendly against them.

In two weeks' time? Here? Saturday at two o'clock. All up for it?"

Were we? Just a bit! The Mexican wave lasted a tad longer this time.

"So that's it," Hannah said. "Go home, take your kit with you and don't lose it because you'll need it. May the fourteenth."

19

Now you would think this was the happy-ever-after bit for me, wouldn't you? After all, I'd got everything I wanted: I was the goalie in a team. I would be playing against another team in two weeks' time. From September, I would be playing against other teams every week. Magic, our Maurice!

But you know how I always get nervous before football practice? Well, in the fortnight leading up to the match I managed to outdo myself. Big time. I couldn't sleep. I couldn't eat. I felt as sick as not one but a whole bunch of parrots. Even Mum noticed, and that's saying something.

"I'm cold," I said on the morning of the match.

"What? It's lovely and warm today. The sun's out. It's glorious."

"I'm cold," I repeated and shivered just to prove it.

She put her hand on my head and scowled. "Hmm. You are running a temperature, sweetheart. I think you might have to give this one a miss."

"No," I mumbled, but I didn't exactly protest.

Dad soon put the kibosh on that idea. "What? Give it a miss? Never! She'll be fine once she walks out onto that pitch. Come on, petal. Up and at 'em." He slapped me on the back and told me to pack my kit.

Mum drove and Dad chatted to me about matches he'd played in at my age, so by the time we arrived in Lornton I was feeling a smidge better, but when Mum pulled up at the ground she couldn't find a parking space. The car park was full, and there were already dozens of parents and kids standing on the touchline. Among them I recognized Petra's mum and dad and her sister, Charlotte, and near to them Mrs Woolcock was standing with Mr

Woolcock. Dotted among the parents were loads of the Parrs players and some of the lads from the Under 10s team. Nightmare! If they were watching I was bound to drop even the easy balls that came to me!

Mum had to reverse all the way back to the main road and park there. I would have run away, if my legs hadn't felt like jelly beans.

I joined everybody in the noisy changing rooms and tried to find a corner where I could hide. Talk about Mission Impossible. Petra immediately came up to me and pulled a goofy face, and Tabinda wanted a high five.

"I'm really nervous!" I heard Holly say.

"Me too," Petra agreed.

"It's only a friendly," Katie said, "so just go out there and enjoy yourselves. Remember, Southfields are feeling just as nervous as you are. More, I bet, seeing as they're away from home."

"You'll soon forget the crowd, so don't worry

about them…" Hannah told us.

Easy for her to say! I glanced down at my brand-new goalkeeper's gloves lying in my lap. My stomach began to churn. The feeling of wanting to throw up increased by ten billion. How embarrassing would that be? Splattering the floor with puke? Or, worse, doing it outside on the pitch in front of everyone. Double nightmare!

Goosepimples puckered my arms and I felt clammy all over. When Hannah gave her pep talk her voice sounded as if it was coming from a long, long way away. "You all know your positions? Amy, you're OK swapping with Holly at half-time?" she asked.

"I suppose so," Amy muttered.

"OK. That just leaves me to give out the captain's armband. I hope you'll all agree it can only go to one person… Megan."

I felt an elbow dig into my ribs. "Meggo!" Petra said. "You're the captain! Go girlfriend!"

I couldn't look up. My head felt as heavy as a

balloon filled with sand. People began to whisper to each other.

"Hey, Megan," a voice called to me. It seemed far away.

I was aware of Hannah squatting in front of me. "You OK?"

I nodded OK first, then shook my head.

"Pre-match nerves?"

I nodded again.

"She always got them before practice at school, but I've never seen her this bad," Tabinda told her.

"Me neither," Petra added.

"It's good to feel tense," Hannah said to me. "It shows how much it means to you. Here, take this." She prodded something into my hand.

My eyes were a bit blurry and at first I thought it was a hanky but then I saw white skulls on a red background. "Your bandana?" I asked. There was a lump in my throat the size of a satsuma.

Hannah smiled at me. "No, *your* bandana. It's like mine, only smaller; I made it for you from some material I had left over. Wear it; it'll take all those nerves away."

"That shade so does not go with ginger hair," I heard Amy mutter as she walked past.

"Shut your mouth! She looks better than you any day!"

When I heard that, I managed to raise my head a little. I saw Jenny-Jane Bayliss, her angry face about half a centimetre from Amy's, her fist curled and ready. Heck! We hadn't even had our first friendly yet and I was bottling out of the match and two players were having domestics! I groaned and shut my eyes tight.

"I'm not saying I'm prettier, I'm just giving some fashion advice," Amy retorted. "Not that it's any of your business, Jenny-Jane!"

"I'll give your big nose some fashion advice in a minute!" Jenny-Jane threatened.

"Whoa! Time out, you two!" Katie said, diving in between them.

"Come on, Amy," said Eve, grabbing her arm

and pulling her away. "Let's warm up."

Hannah patted my knee. "Take a couple of minutes. I'll see you out there."

"I'll stay," Petra said. "I'll see she's OK."

"Good girl," Hannah told her.

20

The changing rooms were suddenly quiet and still. I don't know if that made things better or worse. "I can't play," I whispered to Petra.

"But it's your dream come true," Petra said.

"I know, but I can't go out there. I'm too nervous."

"Nervous? Megan! If you can stand up to that horrible Gary Browne you can do anything."

"I just feel so sick."

"Hey, come and look at this!"

I glanced across the changing rooms to see Tabinda standing at the door. I hadn't realized she was still there.

She turned and grinned, waving me across. "Come here! You've got to see this!"

"I can't."

"You've got to!" she said, her voice stern.

Tabinda is the least bossy person I know. I blinked.

"Come on!" she repeated.

"OK," I said. Somehow I managed to walk the few strides to the open doorway.

"Look!" Tabinda pointed.

"What?"

"There! Over there next to my dad!"

On the far side of the field Mr Shah was talking and laughing with guess who? Mr Glasshouse. Now I really would throw up! "What's *he* doing here?" I asked.

"I invited him after training last week," Tabinda said. "I told him all about how you got the team together."

"Oh." I had stopped going to his practice sessions now I had the Parsnips. These days I only saw Mr Glasshouse when he took assemblies and talked about the magic of recycling.

"He was impressed."

I shrugged. I didn't actually care whether he was impressed or not. All I cared about was keeping my breakfast in my stomach and not splattering it all over the floor.

"Megan! Look! Look at what he's wearing!" Petra laughed.

I squinted. "Is he…? Is that…?"

"Yep. Mr Glasshouse really is wearing fairy wings and a tiara!" Tabinda squawked.

"No way!"

"Way! He said he would be delighted to come and watch the future England goalkeeper in action, so I told him I hoped he'd dress appropriately. I kind of meant in an England shirt but, you know, whatever!"

I laughed. Oh, Mr Glasshouse! So he *had* noticed that day! Did I look as daft as that? No wonder he had ignored me. He'd done right to ignore me, too. I'd been acting like a brat. He was the coach – it was up to him to choose his team. Everyone else had waited until Years Five and Six to represent the school – including his son, Jack. I could have waited too. But then again, if I had, I wouldn't be here today. That was down to Mr Glasshouse, too, for suggesting a girls' team in the first place. I sighed and when I did, I realized my stomach cramps had disappeared. Just like that! It must have been the magic fairy dust from those wings or something!

"I guess I'd better get my gloves on," I said.

"About time," Petra agreed.

"Thanks a bunch!" I strode back to the bench and pulled the gloves on. My heart raced. I felt energy surge through my hands and up my arms. I hoped I'd have the chance to do one of my special dives! Then I realized Hannah's bandana was still lying there on the bench. I would do one of my special dives, just for her! "Oh! Will you do my bandana up for me?" I asked Petra.

"Yes, captain." She smirked, and fastened it in a tight knot.

"Now give me some fashion advice, because you know how much I care about fashion. Does the bandana so clash with my hair?"

"It so does!"

"Wicked!"

Taking a deep breath, I walked out of the changing rooms and into the sunshine.

Final Whistle

Well, that's it from me and Girls FC. Told you I was only going to explain how we started, didn't I? I hope you've enjoyed hearing about the early days. It's been great for me remembering it all again.

I can't believe I almost didn't play against Southfields after all the fuss I'd made about getting the team together in the first place! I think it was just too much to take in. I still get nervous before a match, but nothing like on that day. Silly really because in the end I hardly had anything to do. We won quite easily. In fact at half-time everyone agreed to stop keeping score because it wasn't fair on Southfields. Their

coach told Hannah she couldn't believe
we were only starting out as we seemed
so confident. It's a good job she
hadn't seen me earlier in the changing
rooms!

I am going to hand over to Petra
now. She'll continue the story of
the Parsnips by telling you about
the summer tournament we were involved
in before the season started.

Enjoy!

Love and penalty saves,
Megan F xxx

More from Girls F.C.

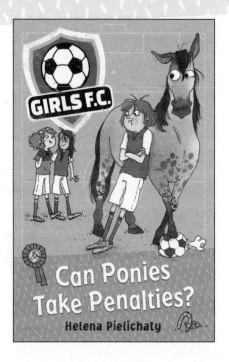

Petra can't wait to play in her first football tournament. While she's not exactly the best defender, it's great spending time with her friend Megan — the team captain.

But the big match clashes with her sister's show-jumping event and, as usual, Charlotte (and her dumb ponies) are her mum's number one priority...

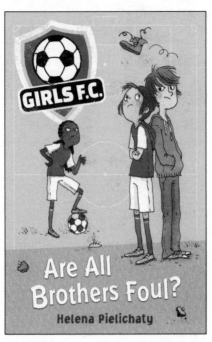

GIRLS F.C.

Are All Brothers Foul?

Helena Pielichaty

Lucy loves football — it's what she lives
for. But her older brother Harry has been
acting up since their parents' divorce
and his moods are making things tense.

Lucy tries to be the peacemaker, but when
Harry's bad behaviour spills over into her
football she knows it's time to make a stand.

More from Girls F.C.

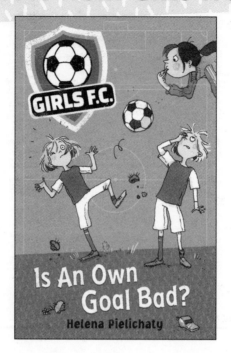

GIRLS F.C.

Is An Own Goal Bad?

Helena Pielichaty

Twins Daisy and Dylan adore playing football, but they never make it to practice on time and their antics on and off the pitch are beginning to annoy their teammates.

When Megan, the captain, tells the twins she is unhappy with their match-reports they ask their Scottish granny for help. Luckily, she knows just how to turn things around…